# WHERE IS DENNIS DeYOUNG?

This special edition of *Where Is Dennis DeYoung?* is limited to one hundred numbered copies signed by the authors.

This is copy __43__ of 100

Gerry Schoenneman

Dan Burns

# WHERE IS DENNIS DeYOUNG?

## An Original Short Film Screenplay

### Gerry Schoenneman
### &
### Dan Burns

Chicago Arts Press

Copyright © 2020 by Gerry Schoenneman and Dan Burns

All rights reserved, including the right to reproduce this book or portions thereof in any form whatsoever. This book is a work of fiction. Any references to historical events, real people, or real places are used fictitiously. Other names, characters, places, and events are products of the author's imagination, and any resemblance to actual events or places or persons, living or dead, is entirely coincidental.

Cover art and illustrations by Kelly Maryanski

Book design by Salvatore Marchetti

Published and printed in the United States of America by

CHICAGO ARTS PRESS

www.chicagoartspress.com

10 9 8 7 6 5 4 3 2 1

First Edition

Based on a true story.

One of the names has been changed to protect the guilty.

# INTRODUCTION

By Gerry Schoenneman

I'm sort of a wack job. Shit continuously rolls off my tongue. My wife calls my verbal spurts "lightning bolts."

This story is the result of one of those lightning bolts. It's based on my chance encounter with Styx guitarist James Young. In June 2012, I attended a concert in Chicago with friends. The bands included Styx, REO Speedwagon, and Ted Nugent. After a full afternoon and evening comprised of drinking, debauchery, and the show, we decided to close out the night in the hotel bar. Unbeknownst to us, we were staying at the same hotel as the bands. Back at the hotel, I entered the elevator and in walked James Young. I was floored, buzzed, and ready to make a fool of myself. That's where the story starts.

The rest of the story was developed with a good friend of mine, Dan Burns, an accomplished author of books, plays, poetry, and scripts. He also happens to have a good memory. Lucky me. Dan and I share a passion for fly fishing and take many trips each year to a property I own in Wisconsin. It has a cabin (actually a barn), a fire pit, whiskey, and a trout stream. Oh yeah, and there's a tavern just down the road—all you need for a four-day hiatus.

On a recent fishing trip, Dan and I were hanging with the locals at the tavern, pouring down a few Jack and Cokes. As usual, after a couple, I started on one of my "lightning bolts," running my mouth about how we need to make past wrongs right. I used the James Young example as a case in point. After what seemed like a dozen or so drinks later, we made our way back to the barn to continue our barrage of excess. That's where the rest of the story came to light. With the help of a blazing fire, unlimited drinks, and blaring music (our late-night MO), our creative juices started to flow—if you want to call it that. Until about 4:00 a.m., I went on and on about how this James Young story could have played out. Meanwhile, Dan listened intently, laughed hysterically (thank you), and pitched in his two cents. It was one of many classic evenings spent at the barn.

By morning, I had forgotten most of the story. But Dan hadn't. Within a couple of days, he had it all down on paper. My man!

# HOW TO READ A SCREENPLAY

The story you are about to enjoy is presented in screenplay format. This format facilitates the movie-making process by focusing on the elements most important to the director and cast in terms of creating the story visually. It also mimics for the reader the experience of watching a movie by including only visible or audible elements.

The screenplay is a series of scenes. The key elements of each scene are the time and place, a brief description of the action, the characters, and the dialogue.

The first line of each scene is presented in ALL CAPS, so it's easy to identify when a new scene begins. Let's look at the first line of our screenplay:

EXT. THE ARCADA THEATRE – ST. CHARLES, IL – NIGHT

This line tells you that the scene is occurring outside (exterior) by the Arcada Theatre in St. Charles, Illinois, at night. EXT means exterior, and INT means interior, or inside.

Within each scene are brief descriptions of the characters and what they're doing—the action. Here's an example from the second scene:

A LIVE STYX CONCERT IS IN PROGRESS.

TERRY SKOONERMAN (50) is standing in the crowd bobbing his head and pumping his fist while watching and listening to the band. He has stringy shoulder-length gray-blond hair and a scruffy beard and is wearing black-framed glasses, a black Styx T-shirt, and jeans.

There are a couple of reasons why ALL CAPS might appear in a scene. In this example, the concert is a detail that the writers are suggesting the director include, either visually or audibly or both. The reader can imagine live concert footage appearing on the movie screen of their mind.

You'll also see ALL CAPS when a character is introduced. Here, we're introduced to our protagonist, Terry Skoonerman, who is fifty years old and enjoying the concert. We also learn what Terry is wearing. Can you picture him? Good!

When the scene is set and the action begins, the characters step in to speak their lines. Each character name is centered on the page and capitalized. Beneath the name is the dialogue—the part of the story that he must tell you. This is an example from the fifth scene:

TERRY
Excuse me, gents, I need to see a man about a dog.

Here is our protagonist again. He feels compelled to share with his friends, and the readers, what he must do. You may see (O.S.) next to a character's name, which means that the character is off-screen. We can hear them but cannot see them.

As with any story, YOUR IMAGINATION is a key aspect of the experience. Visualize the places and the characters, listen to what the characters say, and make yourself a part of the story. Enjoy!

# WHERE IS DENNIS DeYOUNG?

EXT. THE ARCADA THEATRE – ST. CHARLES, IL – NIGHT

ON THE MARQUEE: STYX – LIVE – ONE NIGHT ONLY.

The street is crowded with cars. Twenty excited FANS (various ages) are entering the theatre.

SUPERIMPOSE: "JUNE 2012"

INT. THE ARCADA THEATRE – NIGHT

A LIVE STYX CONCERT IS IN PROGRESS.

TERRY SKOONERMAN (50) is standing in the crowd bobbing his head and pumping his fist while watching and listening to the band. He has stringy shoulder-length gray-blond hair and a scruffy beard and is wearing black-framed glasses, a black Styx T-shirt, and jeans. His THREE FRIENDS (50s), dressed similarly but acting less animated, surround him. As the song ends, they high-five each other.

EXT. THE ARCADA THEATRE – NIGHT

A stream of FANS (various ages) are exiting the theatre. Terry exits the venue by himself, beaming, the happiest guy in the world. His friends exit the theatre. More high-fives all around.

EXT. HOTEL BAKER – ST. CHARLES, IL – NIGHT

Terry and his friends enter the hotel, one at a time, through the revolving door. Terry is last, checking his phone and not paying attention, and he gets pinched between the moving door and the door frame. He winces in pain but quickly recovers, pushes his glasses back up, and enters.

INT. HOTEL BAKER – BAR – NIGHT

Terry's friends are sitting at the bar. Terry is standing beside them. He's intoxicated, loud, and obnoxious, sharing his memories of the concert. They each drink a shot. Terry excuses himself to use the restroom.

> TERRY
> Excuse me, gents, I need to see a man about a dog.

His friends look at each other and shake their heads.

> FRIEND ONE
> Yeah, whatever, dude.

Terry leaves the bar area.

INT. HOTEL BAKER – HALLWAY – NIGHT

At the restroom door, while reaching for the door handle, Terry turns and sees JAMES "JY" YOUNG (62), guitarist, singer, and songwriter for the rock band Styx, waiting for the elevator. James Young has shoulder-length blond hair and is wearing a stylish suit with an open-collared shirt.

The elevator door opens. James Young enters the elevator.

Terry rushes over and steps into the elevator, and the door closes.

INT. HOTEL BAKER – ELEVATOR – NIGHT

Terry and James Young are standing in the elevator. Terry is awestruck, his eyes bulging and upper lip quivering. He turns and gazes at James Young, who looks over curiously.

                    TERRY
            Uh, great show tonight.

                 JAMES YOUNG
            Thanks.

Terry relaxes a bit, takes a deep breath.

                    TERRY
            Your guitar playing was awesome.

                 JAMES YOUNG
            Thanks.

Terry nods and pushes his glasses up, not sure what to say next.

                    TERRY
            My name's Terry. Terry Skoonerman.

James Young opens his mouth, about to speak. Terry is instantly excited.

               TERRY (CONT'D)
            I've been a fan of yours for years. I can't
            believe it. I'm in an elevator with Dennis
            DeYoung!

James Young frowns.

                 JAMES YOUNG
            I think you're mistaken.

                    TERRY
            No, no, I get it. You don't want people to
            know who you are, don't need the atten-
            tion. I get it. You want to be incognito.

> TERRY (CONT'D)
> Don't worry, I won't tell.

James Young shakes his head and sighs in exasperation. The elevator door opens. As he steps out—

> TERRY (CONT'D)
> Unbelievable. Dennis DeYoung. You're Dennis DeYoung!

James Young, in the hallway, turns and glares at Terry. The elevator door closes.

CLOSE-UP: TERRY, SMILING.

> TERRY (CONT'D)
> Dennis DeYoung. What a night!

INT. HOTEL BAKER – BAR – NIGHT

Terry walks into the bar and approaches his friends.

> TERRY
> You're not going to believe who I just saw.

> FRIEND ONE
> Shut up and drink your shot. You're two behind.

Terry drinks a shot, grimaces.

> FRIEND TWO
> One more.

Terry drinks his second shot, coughs.

TERRY

You're not going to believe it. I was on my way to the restroom—

FRIEND ONE

I thought you were going to get a dog?

The other two friends chuckle. Terry is confused.

TERRY

Huh? What? Oh, cut it out. So, listen to this, just as I was about to open the door to the restroom, I turned and saw Dennis DeYoung getting into the elevator.

FRIEND THREE

What are you talking about?

TERRY

So I figured my piss could wait, and I ran over and jumped into the elevator with him.

FRIEND ONE

With Dennis DeYoung? The famous singer?

TERRY

Yeah. From the concert tonight. It was just him and me, and I introduced myself and told him I was a big fan. I wasn't sure what else to say, so I said, "I can't believe I'm in an elevator with Dennis DeYoung!"

FRIEND TWO
And what did he say?

TERRY
He said I was mistaken, which I get because he was trying to be all incognito, didn't want everyone to know who he was and start bothering him. I get it.

FRIEND THREE
I don't think you do.

TERRY
What a night. The best concert of my life, and then I get to meet my favorite guitarist, Dennis DeYoung!

FRIEND THREE
What did he look like?

TERRY
He looked like Dennis DeYoung—you know, tall, long blond hair, very cool. We saw him play at the concert tonight!

FRIEND ONE
You idiot. That was James Young, not Dennis DeYoung.

Terry's eyes cross, and his head twitches.

TERRY
Huh?

> FRIEND TWO
> Dennis DeYoung, the original singer of
> Styx, left the band over ten years ago.

> TERRY
> Wait. What?

> FRIEND ONE
> You got the name wrong, you fucking
> idiot. That was James Young!

Terry's friends laugh while punching his arms and mussing up his hair.

CLOSE-UP OF TERRY, HIS EXPRESSION WORRIED AND EYES WATERY.

> TERRY
> James Young. Oh, no.

Terry deflates, crushed, and his head drops.

INT. TERRY'S APARTMENT – CHICAGO – LIVING ROOM – NIGHT

Terry is sitting in the recliner in his small man-cave apartment, distraught and weary, listening to his old Styx records, which are spread out on his lap. His phone is on the arm of the chair. A box of tissues is on the side table, along with a small pile of used, crumpled tissues.

Terry picks up the phone and reads the displayed article.

CLOSE-UP: NEWSPAPER ARTICLE – CHICAGO ENQUIRER – OCTOBER 12, 1999. HEADLINE: "DENNIS DEYOUNG LEAVES THE FAMED ROCK BAND STYX."

Terry sighs.

TIME LAPSE OVER THREE DAYS: Terry is sitting in the chair, his beard growing, his hygiene deteriorating, his expression appearing wearier. The mess of soda cans, used tissues, and dishes piles up around him as each day passes.

INT. TERRY'S APARTMENT – LIVING ROOM – DAY – THREE DAYS LATER

Terry is sleeping in the chair. He wakes up and scans his surroundings wearily. He looks down at the Styx albums in his lap and caresses them lovingly.

FLASHBACKS: THE STYX CONCERT; MEETING JAMES YOUNG ON THE ELEVATOR; HIS FRIENDS AT THE BAR, LAUGHING AT HIM.

> TERRY
> James Young. Oh, no. I can't believe I called him Dennis DeYoung.

Terry gets an idea. He raises his eyebrows, smiles, and lifts an index finger as though pointing to the ceiling. He stands up and walks to the stereo.

At the turntable, Terry holds the sleeve of Styx's album *Paradise Theatre* and stares at it. Then he puts the record on the turntable, plays it, and turns up the volume.

Terry stands before the wall mirror.

WE SEE TERRY'S REFLECTION IN THE MIRROR.

THE STYX SONG "SNOWBLIND" PLAYS: *Mirror, mirror on the wall / The face you've shown me scares me so / Thought that I could call your bluff / But now the lines are clear enough / Life's not pretty, even though / I tried so hard to make it so / Mornings are such cold distress / How did I ever get into this mess . . .*

Terry's reflection in the mirror blurs, becomes wavy.

CUT TO:

EXT. A SNOWY MOUNTAINTOP – DAY

THE SONG "SNOWBLIND" CONTINUES TO PLAY.

James Young and Terry are standing on the peak of the mountain, close to and facing each other, their hair flowing in the wind, dressed only in loincloths and wearing Viking helmets.

CLOSE-UP OF TERRY, WHO IS GAZING LONGINGLY AT JAMES YOUNG. CLOSE-UP OF JAMES YOUNG, WHO IS GAZING LONGINGLY AT TERRY.

Snow falls, first lightly and then more heavily as the seconds pass.

James Young slowly slides away backward. As he reaches the edge of the peak, Terry reaches out a hand with an expression of desperation.

James Young fades away down the mountainside then disappears.

CLOSE-UP OF TERRY: A tear drips down his cheek.

CUT TO:

INT. TERRY'S APARTMENT – LIVING ROOM – DAY

Back in his apartment, Terry is still in front of the mirror. His blurry, wavy reflection becomes clear.

TERRY'S REFLECTION IN THE MIRROR. His eyes are wet and red. He wipes away the tears from his cheeks.

> TERRY
> I must fix this. I have to make it right. I must redeem myself in the eyes of James Young!

Terry turns from the mirror and walks away.

INT. TERRY'S APARTMENT – LIVING ROOM – DAY

Terry is at his desk, in front of his computer. He's reading an advertisement displayed on the screen.

COMPUTER SCREEN: "JAMES YOUNG OF STYX TO VISIT CHRISTIAN YOUTH SUMMER CAMP."

Terry's eyes open wide as he experiences a moment of devout realization.

> TERRY
> Redemption! This is my chance!

Terry taps a key on the computer, and the printer on the desk produces an application. He grabs the application, gets up from his desk, and walks toward the kitchen.

INT. TERRY'S APARTMENT – KITCHEN – DAY

Terry is sitting at the kitchen table, a sandwich and a glass of milk in front of him, filling out the Christian Youth Summer Camp application.

CLOSE-UP OF LINE ON APPLICATION: CAMPER AGE:

Terry writes his answer on the blank line.

CLOSE-UP OF LINE ON APPLICATION: CAMPER AGE: 17

Terry writes in three other responses.

CLOSE-UP OF LINE ON APPLICATION: ETHNICITY: CATHOLIC (I THINK)

CLOSE-UP OF LINE ON APPLICATION: HAIR COLOR: GRAY

CLOSE-UP OF LINE ON APPLICATION: HOBBIES: I LIKE TO PLAY WITH CLAY AND READ MAGAZINES

Terry signs and folds the application, sticks it into an envelope, and licks and seals the envelope.

He holds the envelope in both hands as though it's a precious artifact, looks down at it, and smiles.

EXT. CHRISTIAN YOUTH SUMMER CAMP – WISCONSIN – FLAGPOLE – DAY – WEEKS LATER

It's opening day at Christian Youth Summer Camp. A group of one hundred CAMPERS (14–17) stand around a flagpole dressed in camper uniforms of shorts and T-shirts.

Terry is standing in the middle of the group, a foot taller than everyone else. He's wearing the same outfit as the other campers, but his shorts are too short and his T-shirt too tight. His striped tube socks come up to his knees, and he's wearing his very old high-top sneakers.

The campers bow their heads. The CAMP CHAPLAIN (50) leads the group in a prayer. Terry looks up with an expression of elation.

TWO FEMALE CAMPERS (14–17) are standing next to Terry.

>FEMALE CAMPER ONE
>What is he doing here?

The other female camper shrugs.

EXT. CHRISTIAN YOUTH SUMMER CAMP – FISHING DOCK – DAY

Terry is fishing off the dock with FOUR MALE CAMPERS (14–17) standing behind him. He hooks one of the campers in the arm.

>CAMPER ONE
>Watch it, you doofus!

A camper covers his mouth and whispers to the other campers.

>CAMPER TWO
>Is he a Narc?

The other campers shrug.

EXT. CHRISTIAN YOUTH SUMMER CAMP – FOREST – DAY

Terry is alone and building a campfire. He douses the wood with a full bottle of lighter fluid then lights it with a match. An exploding ball of flames forces Terry backward, stumbling.

The flames settle down and the smoke clears. Terry is standing by the fire, dejected, his face covered with soot, his hair and eyebrows singed.

INT. CHRISTIAN YOUTH SUMMER CAMP – MUSIC ROOM – DAY

Terry is sitting in a circle with a group of TEN CAMPERS (14–17) in a music-making session. In the middle of a slow, religious song, he stands with his electric guitar and seizes control of the song with an animated, raging guitar solo. The other campers stop playing and watch him with wonder and contempt.

INT. CHRISTIAN YOUTH SUMMER CAMP – AUDITORIUM ENTRANCE – DAY

CLOSE-UP OF POSTER FOR THE JAMES YOUNG EVENT: CAMPER CONCERT THIS FRIDAY! FEATURING JAMES YOUNG, THE VOICE AND GUITAR OF THE ROCK BAND STYX!

INT. CHRISTIAN YOUTH SUMMER CAMP – AUDITORIUM – DAY

A group meeting. All the campers are sitting in the auditorium's folding chairs. The CAMP LEADER (45) stands before the campers.

CAMP LEADER
All right, campers, as you know, we have a very special guest. James Young, from the rock band Styx, will be joining us for our camper concert event this Friday. Does anyone have a suggestion for a unique way that we can welcome him?

A MALE CAMPER (15) is picking his nose, appearing clueless.

A FEMALE CAMPER (16) is reclining in her seat, bored and uninterested, twirling a finger in her hair.

FEMALE CAMPER
James who?

The other campers look around at each other, perplexed. Terry raises his hand.

CAMP LEADER
Yes, Terry?

TERRY
James "JY" Young, the one and only, the guitarist, singer, and songwriter for quite possibly the greatest rock band in the world, Styx.

The campers look at each other, unimpressed.

CAMP LEADER
Do you have a suggestion, Terry?

TERRY
Do I ever. We should present him with a Lifetime Achievement Award.

The camp leader nods in approval.

INT. CHRISTIAN YOUTH SUMMER CAMP – AUDITORIUM – NIGHT

The campers, some excited, some already bored, are in their seats waiting for the camper concert to begin. The camp leader walks to center stage and grabs the microphone.

Terry is standing off to one side at the edge of the stage, excited, hands together and ready to clap.

> CAMP LEADER
> Ladies and gentlemen, before we begin the concert, we are pleased to award our first-ever Lifetime Achievement Award to a guitarist, singer, and songwriter who is best known for playing lead guitar in the American rock band Styx. Please welcome to the stage Mr. Dennis DeYoung!

The crowd erupts, everyone clapping and cheering.

Terry is shocked that the leader said the wrong name. CLOSE-UP OF TERRY'S FACE. HE SPEAKS IN SLOW-MOTION.

> TERRY
> Oh, fudge. Not again.

James Young walks onto the stage, appearing disgusted at the name mix-up, shaking his head.

Terry is clapping wildly in the hope of making the situation better.

                    TERRY (CONT'D)
          Woo! Woo!

Terry whistles and claps as loud and as fast as he can.

James Young approaches the camp leader, accepts the award reluctantly, and stands before the microphone with a disappointed expression.

Terry stops clapping, and the crowd quiets.

                    JAMES YOUNG
          My name is not DeYoung. It's just Young.
          James Young.

James Young walks off the stage.

Terry is standing motionless, a worried expression on his face.

                    TERRY
          James Young. Oh, no.

Everyone in the auditorium looks around, wondering what just happened.

INT. CHRISTIAN YOUTH SUMMER CAMP – AUDITORIUM – BACKSTAGE – NIGHT

James Young pulls out his phone. CLOSE-UP: THE UBER APP. He taps his phone a few times. He exits the rear stage door, slamming it closed behind him.

A burning lantern, hanging on the wall next to the door, drops from its hook and falls into a trash can, which ignites. Hanging curtains next to the can ignite, and the flames crawl up the wall.

EXT. CHRISTIAN YOUTH SUMMER CAMP – AUDITORIUM – REAR STAGE DOOR – NIGHT

James Young is standing next to the rear stage door, his back against the wall. He's holding his trophy in one hand, his phone in the other. While he's staring at his phone, it beeps. He walks around the corner of the building and toward the street to meet his Uber driver.

EXT. CHRISTIAN YOUTH SUMMER CAMP – AUDITORIUM – NIGHT

An Uber car pulls up in front of the auditorium building. The UBER DRIVER (25) steps out.

UBER DRIVER
Mr. DeYoung! Dennis DeYoung!

The driver looks around, searching, and gets no response.

James Young is about thirty yards from the street when he hears the Uber driver. He stops and shakes his head, again disgusted.

JAMES YOUNG
Unbelievable.

James Young turns and walks toward the bordering forest.

INT. CHRISTIAN YOUTH SUMMER CAMP – AUDITORIUM – NIGHT

Inside the auditorium, smoke billows out from the stage and into the crowd. Pandemonium ensues. Campers are screaming and scrambling to exit the auditorium.

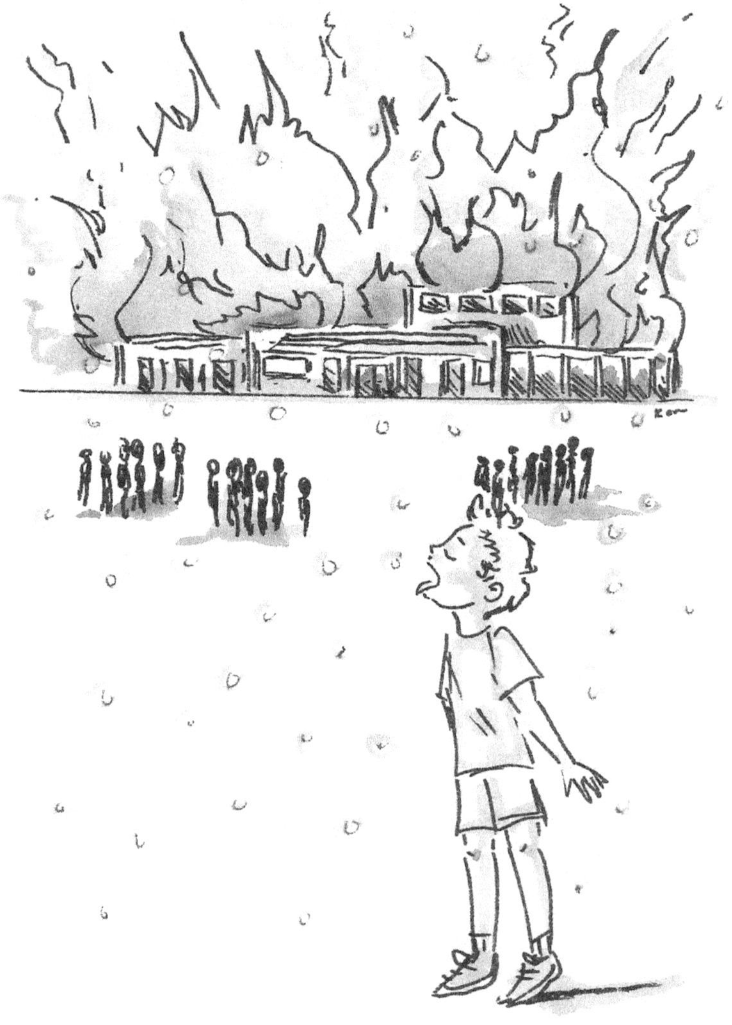

Two campers are trapped under a pile of chairs, yelling for help.

EXT. CHRISTIAN YOUTH SUMMER CAMP – AUDITORIUM – NIGHT

Terry exits and stands outside the building, scared and breathing heavily.

SCREAMS FOR HELP EMERGE FROM INSIDE THE AUDITORIUM.

Terry poses like Superman, sticking out his chest, appearing newly energized with bravery. He runs back and re-enters the building.

The campers are gathered in front of the auditorium, comforting each other, their gazes focused on the front door.

Terry exits the building with a camper under each arm. Everyone gathers around and congratulates him.

He drops the kids on the ground as though they are sacks of flour. He looks over the heads of the campers and scans the surrounding area.

TERRY
I need to find James Young.

Terry runs off toward the rear of the auditorium building.

The sky turns dark and menacing, and snow begins to fall. The campers look up to the sky and at each other in amazement. A camper sticks out his tongue to catch the falling flakes.

EXT. CHRISTIAN YOUTH SUMMER CAMP – FOREST – NIGHT

James Young is walking through the forest with his award, depressed and contemplative. He doesn't notice the falling and blowing snow.

EXT. CHRISTIAN YOUTH SUMMER CAMP – AUDITORIUM – NIGHT

The Uber driver is standing beside his parked car in front of the burning auditorium building. He looks up and around at the falling snow.

          UBER DRIVER
     What the hell?

FROM THE RADIO OF THE UBER DRIVER'S CAR, A MAN'S VOICE: "WE HAVE REPORTS OF A FREAK SNOWSTORM MOVING ACROSS THE STATE OF WISCONSIN. PLEASE BE ADVISED THAT ROAD CONDITIONS ARE TREACHEROUS."

The Uber driver scratches his head.

          UBER DRIVER (CONT'D)
     Mr. DeYoung! Dennis DeYoung!

The driver looks around, searching, and gets no response.

EXT. CHRISTIAN YOUTH SUMMER CAMP – FOREST – NIGHT

Still walking through the forest, James Young is looking down at his award, and he trips on a log and falls forward to the ground.

He strikes his head on a rock, rolls down a slope, and is stopped by a tree. With his back up against the tree, he sits motionless, eyes closed.

EXT. CHRISTIAN YOUTH SUMMER CAMP – AUDITORIUM – NIGHT

The Uber driver is standing by his car, looking at his phone with a worried expression.

> UBER DRIVER
> Mr. DeYoung! Mr. DeYoung!

He scans the area.

EXT. CHRISTIAN YOUTH SUMMER CAMP – AUDITORIUM – NIGHT

Terry finds footprints in the grass and newly fallen snow and runs toward the forest.

> UBER DRIVER (O.S.)
> Mr. DeYoung! Mr. Dennis DeYoung!

Terry stops at the edge of the forest, turns around, and glares at the driver, furious.

> TERRY
> His name is James Young, you idiot!

Terry looks up at the falling snow, perplexed. He runs into the forest.

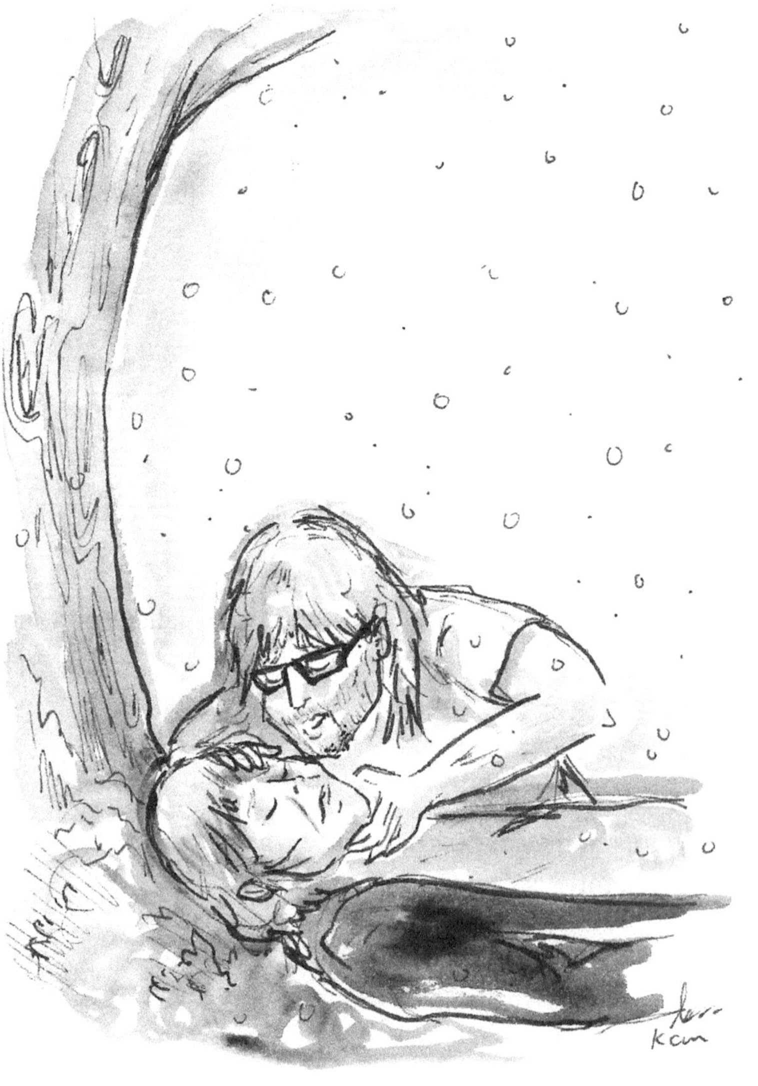

EXT. CHRISTIAN YOUTH SUMMER CAMP – FOREST
– NIGHT

Terry scrambles through the forest, the snow now falling heavily and blowing sideways. He forges on, looking behind trees and scanning the ground for more footprints.

He sees James Young sitting on the ground. He's covered in snow, his back up against a tree, eyes closed. Terry runs to him, kneels, brushes the snow from James Young's face and slaps him a couple of times.

TERRY
James, it's me, Terry. Terry Skoonerman.

James Young doesn't respond. Terry lays James Young on his back, adjusts his head, and bends down to give him mouth-to-mouth. Just as their lips are about to touch, James Young opens his eyes and spits a mouthful of snow into Terry's face.

JAMES YOUNG
Don't even think about it.

Terry holds James Young in his arms, brushes the wet, snowy hair from his face, and comforts him.

UBER DRIVER (O.S.)
Mr. DeYoung! Dennis DeYoung!

James Young is weary, coughs.

JAMES YOUNG
Not DeYoung . . . Just Young.

Terry turns his head toward the Uber driver's voice.

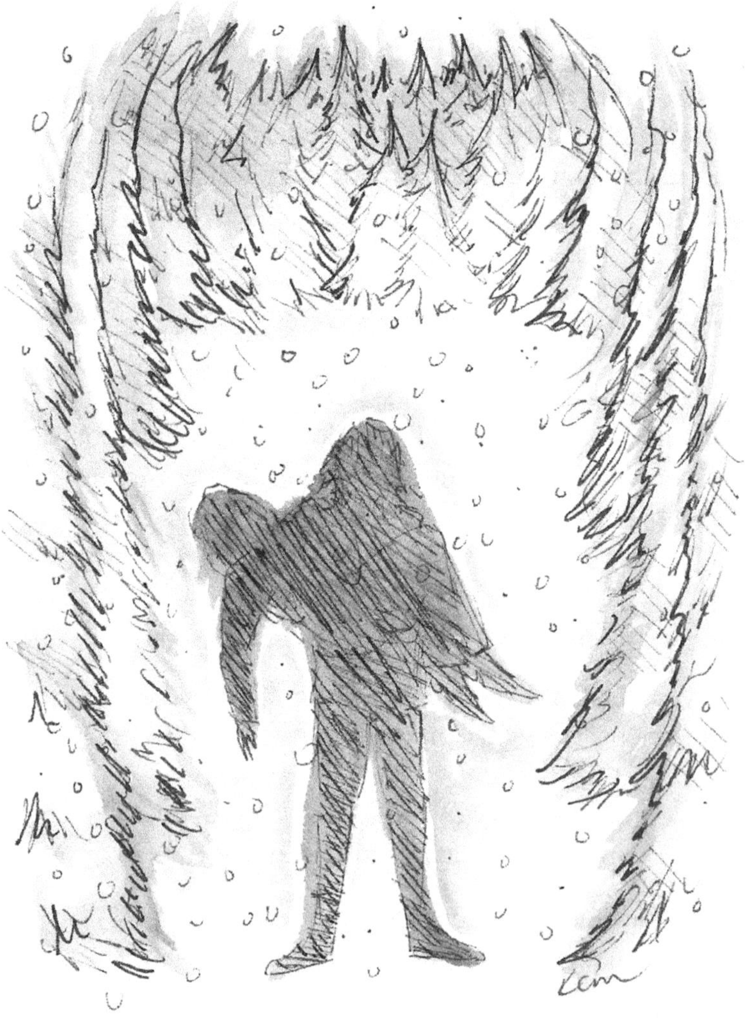

                    TERRY
It's just Young, dammit! James "JY" Young!

                    JAMES YOUNG
You . . .

James Young coughs.

                    TERRY
It's me. Terry.

                    JAMES YOUNG
Terry, you saved my life.

Terry cradles James Young in his arms and rocks him like a child.

EXT. CHRISTIAN YOUTH SUMMER CAMP – AUDITORIUM – NIGHT

The snowfall lightens. Fire trucks are parked on the street, lights flashing. Firefighters are spraying the building's roof with hoses.

The campers are gathered in front of the building, cold and shivering, watching the building burn.

Terry emerges from the forest carrying James Young in his arms.

                                                    CUT TO:


FRONT PAGE OF THE LOCAL NEWSPAPER: "CAMPER SAVES HIS ROCK IDOL." THERE'S A PICTURE OF TERRY IN HIS WET AND DIRTY CAMPER UNIFORM LOADING JAMES YOUNG INTO AN AMBULANCE.

INT. MUSIC VENUE – CHICAGO – NIGHT – WEEKS LATER

A LIVE STYX CONCERT IS IN PROGRESS.

The song ends and the crowd cheers. TOMMY SHAW (58), singer and guitarist of Styx, is standing at center stage before a microphone.

> TOMMY SHAW
> Ladies and gentlemen, on lead guitar
> and vocals: James "JY" Young.

James Young takes a bow. The crowd roars and applauds. He points to a fan in the front row.

Terry is in the front row, wide-eyed and grinning. He points to James Young.

A FAN (50) next to Terry tugs on his arm.

> FAN
> Hey, dude, where's Dennis DeYoung?

> TERRY
> I don't know, and I don't care.

The band plays another song. James Young plays a guitar solo.

Terry, standing in the crowd, is playing a mimicking solo on his air guitar.

The song ends, and Terry raises his arms in triumph.

INT – UBER DRIVER'S CAR – DOWNTOWN CHICAGO – NIGHT

The UBER DRIVER (30) is sitting in his car, which is parked in front of a restaurant. He's playing a game on his phone.

The back door opens and DENNIS DEYOUNG (65), the former lead singer of the rock band Styx, steps in and sits in the back seat.

The Uber driver turns around.

> UBER DRIVER
> Dennis DeYoung?

> DENNIS DEYOUNG
> Yes, I am.

The Uber driver turns back around, puts the car into gear, and drives away.

> FADE TO BLACK.
>
> THE END.

# AFTERWORD

## By Dan Burns

I'll take a story idea any way I can get it.

A story idea can present itself at any time, and it can pop into a person's head based on any number of circumstances: an experience, something heard or read, or a firing of neurons that summons the magic of the conscious and unconscious mind.

Regarding *Where Is Dennis DeYoung?* the idea originated in the mind of my good friend and writing collaborator Gerry Schoenneman. Fortunately, I was there when Gerry's neurons fired, resulting in a grand idea about a man seeking redemption after a name mix-up involving a rock-and-roll musician. Somehow, I was able to remember the story idea, and we subsequently developed and documented the idea as a short film screenplay.

I first met Gerry over thirty years ago as we began our careers as software developers at a Chicago-based health insurance company. We instantly became friends, likely because of our shared interests in music, sports, and excelling at our jobs. As we navigated the many challenges of work and family, our friendship never faltered. Instead, it grew stronger through our sharing of concerts, fishing expeditions, and late-night drinking binges. Although I've never collaborated with anyone on a writing project in my twelve years as a writer until now, it seems logical that I ended up doing so with Gerry.

When we're together, Gerry is always talking. If you know Gerry, then you know what I mean. His endless talking works for me—I love him for it. I'd much rather listen and not be on the hook for coming up with something interesting to say. Plus, he's arguably the funniest guy I know. When we're out together, we're never at a loss for entertainment; he always has a good story to tell.

I must admit that my brain has a filter that I cannot fully control, which allows me to hear but not listen, and I've missed and forgotten many of Gerry's stories—my loss. However, on a late summer evening in September 2018, my filter didn't work.

That evening, at Gerry's property in Southwest Wisconsin, on one of our annual fly-fishing trips, Gerry was in rare storytelling form, the stars were in perfect alignment, and Mnemosyne, the Greek goddess of memory, looked down favorably upon us.

I was back at my office Monday morning, still reeling from the effects of a two-day hangover, and to my surprise, I remembered Gerry's story. I couldn't remember anything else that had been said or done that evening at the barn, but I remembered the story in all its detail and glory. We had agreed that the story would make a great short film, so I quickly typed out a scene outline while the memory was fresh. I laughed as the story developed on the page, and a day later, I had completed a draft of the screenplay.

That's how it is with a good story—it stays with you.

Over several months, Gerry and I worked on the screenplay, laughing throughout the process, to develop it into the story you just read. I hope you enjoyed it as much as we did and had a laugh or two. Maybe it will stay with you too. And, who knows, perhaps we'll all get to see it on the big screen someday.

CPSIA information can be obtained
at www.ICGtesting.com
Printed in the USA
BVHW042343091120
592941BV00009B/35/J